LITTLE FOX AND THE WILD IMAGINATION

WRITTEN BY JORMA TACCONE   ART BY DAN SANTAT

Roaring Brook Press
New York

When Poppa Fox showed up after school, he was surprised to find Little Fox in a bad mood.

"Hey, kiddo! How was school?" asked Poppa Fox.

"Pffffft," said Little Fox.

"I fell off the slide today, and a big kid laughed at me," said Little Fox.
"I don't want to go to school ever again."

"Hmmm. That's rough," Poppa Fox said as he tried to think of something
to cheer up Little Fox.

"Hey, how about we play pretend?"
Poppa Fox suggested.

"Pfffffffffff!" said Little Fox again.

"You're right. No pretending!" said Poppa Fox as he took off running.
"And let's definitely not . . ."

"You feeling better now?" asked Poppa Fox.

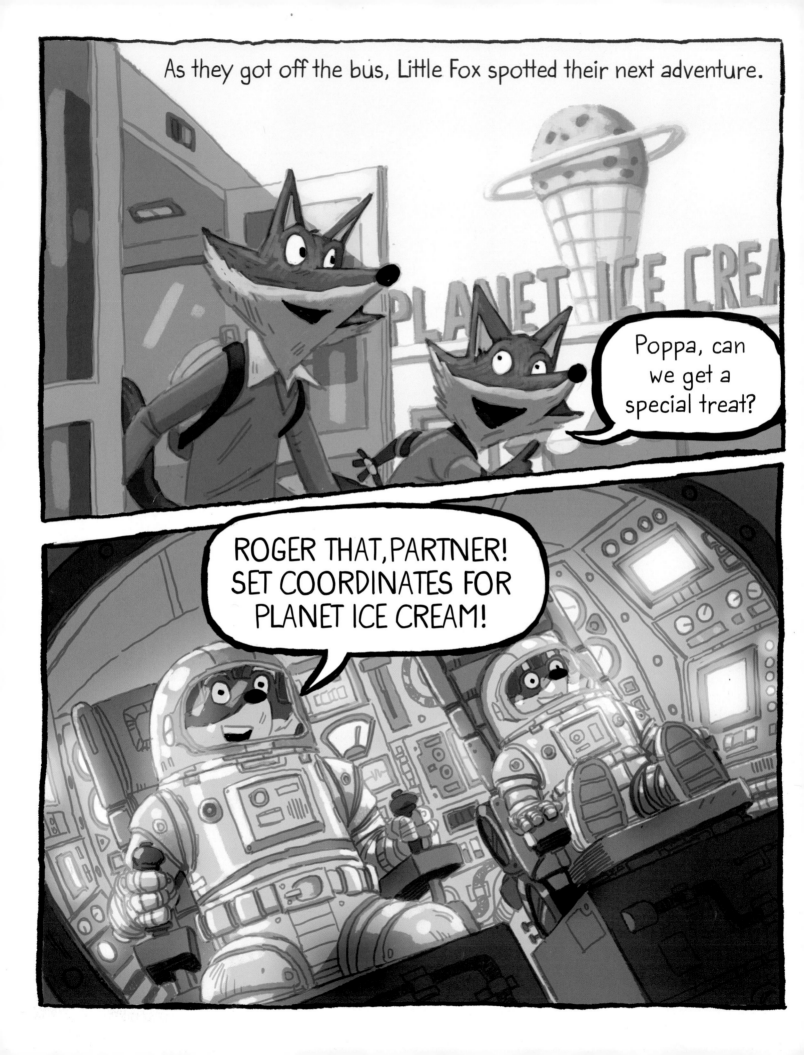

MISSION ACCOMPLISHED, HOUSTON. WE HAVE ONE HAPPY KID, AND WE ARE HEADED HOME TO MAKE DINNER.

Things were going great, but at dinner, their game of pretend took a turn . . .

"Ooh! You should pretend you're a GIANT and eat this whole broccoli forest!" said Poppa Fox. "Wouldn't that be funny?"

"Noooooo!" said Little Fox.

"Let's pretend I'm a robot squid who bashes trees with my TENTACLES!"

Suddenly, Poppa Fox regretted their trip to Planet Ice Cream.

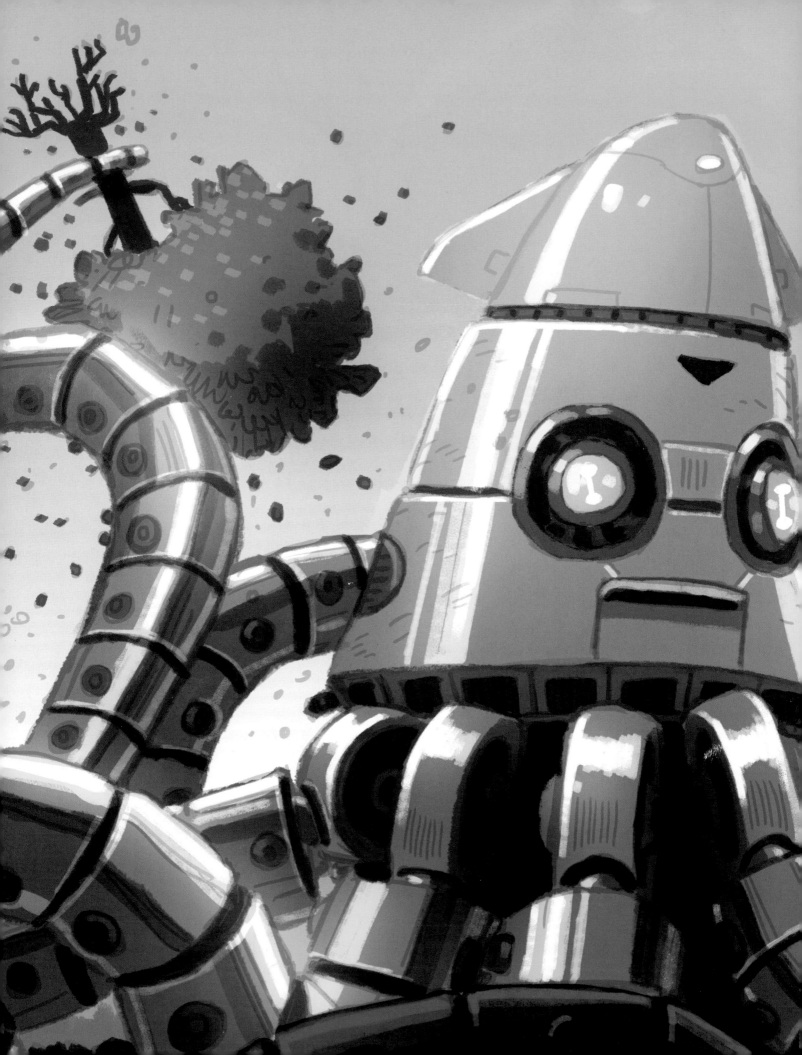

ROBOT SQUID ACTIVATED! DESTROY-ALL-TREES!
OKAY! STOP PRETENDING! WE'RE MAKING A MESS! BATH TIME! IT'S BATH TIME!

Once they were in the bath, Poppa Fox made another big mistake. "Time to wash hair, kiddo."

"NOOO!" cried Little Fox. "We did hair last night! More pretending, you scurvy bad guy!"

"No, no, no! Wait, wait!" said Poppa Fox. But it was too late . . .

"Don't worry. This magic wand will keep us safe in the dark."

"Oh, good. Will it also make you sleepy?" asked Poppa Fox.

"No," whispered Little Fox. "We have to read these books first."

At last, it was bedtime.

"Poppa, can you pick me up from school again tomorrow?" asked Little Fox.

"Sure," said Poppa Fox. "You got it, kiddo."

Good. Because tomorrow, I will blast you off in a rocket and explode you into the sun, you scurvy bad guy.

"I love you, too," said Poppa Fox.